Benny Helps Out

Written and illustrated by
Keren Ludlow and Willy Smax

Orion
Children's Books

First published in Great Britain in 1996
by Orion Children's Books
a division of the Orion Publishing Group Ltd
Orion House
5 Upper St Martin's Lane
London WC2H 9EA

Based on a story from BENNY THE BREAKDOWN TRUCK
Text copyright © Willy Smax 1994, 1996
Illustration copyright © Keren Ludlow 1994, 1996

A catalogue record for this book is available from the British Library
Printed in Italy
ISBN 1 85881 285 2

It was a busy day for
Mike McCannick.

There were lots of cars
waiting to be repaired.

Mike was rushing around
trying to get them all fixed.

Warren Beetle was up on the ramp. His clutch needed adjusting.

Doris Minor had to have her brakes checked.

Francis Ford Popular wanted an oil change.

Alfie Romeo was waiting for a new fanbelt.

Benny the Breakdown Truck was looking on. He felt sorry for Mike. All the cars wanted him at once.

"Hurry up, please," called Alfie.
"My fanbelt is killing me."

"I'm being as quick as I can,"
said Mike, hurrying over to
Alfie with his toolbox.

He tripped up over the wheelbrace,
fell backwards over some oil cans,
and dropped the toolbox.

The tools were scattered
all over the floor.

"Oh dear," said Mike. "It'll take me hours to sort this lot out and find what I need. I'll never get finished."

"What a mess!" said Francis. "It's like living in a scrapyard."

"A scrapyard! You've given me an idea!" said Benny.

And he disappeared
down the road.

By now the cars were
starting to complain.

"I can't wait here
all day with my
bonnet up,"
said Alfie.

"What
about
my
oil?"
said
Francis.

"I'm getting dizzy
up on this
ramp,"
said
Warren.

"My
brakes
are
aching,"
said
Doris.

Poor Mike didn't know what to do.

He couldn't
find his
spanner.

He couldn't
find his
screwdriver.

He looked around the garage.

"Where's Benny?" he asked.

"He went off somewhere,"
said Francis.

Just then, Benny came back.
"Where have you been?"
asked Mike.

"I went to the scrapyard to
borrow a giant magnet,"
said Benny. "Watch this!"

Benny
swung the
powerful
magnet
round
the garage.

The tools began to roll
across the floor.

Then they jumped up
and stuck to the magnet.

"Thanks, Benny!" said Mike.
"Now I can see my tools I'll
be finished in no time."

He found
the right
spanner
to tighten
up Doris's
wheelnuts.

He reached for his screwdriver
and adjusted Warren's clutch.

He changed Francis's oil.

He replaced Alfie's fanbelt.

Soon all the cars were
running smoothly,

and Smallbills Garage
was back in order again.